ADORED

by the

MOUNTAIN MAN

HALLIE BENNETT

PROLOGUE

LUNA

"How long is this going to take?" My mom's disgruntled question pokes a hole in the bubble of pride I've been floating in since learning the Chamber of Commerce wanted to honor me. After helping multiple local businesses launch their websites, someone nominated me for the Emerging Leaders award, and this morning's chamber meeting is when I'll receive the commendation.

A part of me had hoped my mom would be proud of me—would care that her only daughter is being recognized before the entire town of Suitor's Crossing. But her apparent disinterest proves how wrong I'd been to think this time would be different from every other time we're together.

"Meetings are usually an hour. I'm not sure when they'll mention the award, though." Most of the attendees are speaking along the edges of the room with cups of the provided hot coffee in hand. No one seems in a particular hurry to start the meeting early since there are ten minutes before it's officially slated to begin.

Mom huffs in annoyance and pulls out her phone. "Just remember, I have to pick up Bob's groceries at eleven-thirty, so this better not run long. Shouldn't have even come," she mumbles under her breath. "Now you've got me stressed about work."

A guilty flush heats my cheeks as I focus on the bright screen of my own phone, my skin tingling in shame and disappointment. She'd mentioned the odd job when I asked her to come with me last week, but I convinced her to attend anyway, promising it wouldn't interfere with her schedule. Then on the drive here, she brought it up again, deflating my sense of accomplishment even more.

Colors blur on the screen as I bite my tongue and rapidly blink away tears. I should have known she'd ruin this for me.

Everyone comes before you.

Even Bob, a random man in her neighborhood that she somehow agreed to run small errands for. Since my dad died, Mom lives off spousal checks from Veteran Affairs, and to make ends meet, she picks up gigs around town when she feels like it.

They're always at strange times and never pressing, but somehow they become a matter of life or death when one falls during a time I need her. Like when I had surgery for my wisdom teeth and needed a ride home—Mom was an hour late picking me up because she wanted to start a load of laundry for a friend. Or when I booked us a mother/daughter spa package for her birthday, and she told me that another friend asked to be driven to the library.

Every errand is vague with "friends" I don't know, yet they take priority over me.

It was stupid asking her to come today.

But I'll make the same mistake again and again. Because no matter how many times she lets me down, my optimistic personality refuses to let me quit trying—refuses to let me quit with all of my family, really. Relatives who think I'm "weird" or "too much" until a gift-giving occasion where they're the center of attention. Then I'm tolerated enough to receive whatever I bought them.

Geez, this is not how I want to feel before being honored by the Chamber.

A notification appears at the top of my screen, and I eagerly click on it to view my "Music Year Unwrapped." I love insights like these and enjoy the snapshot they provide of who I am.

Music plays once the app opens, spurring me on to quickly lower the volume before someone hears as slides showcase my top artists and my listening personality. "Hey, Mom, look. They deemed me an 'Out of this World Explorer.' Check out the rest of my traits." I offer her my phone, but she ignores my outstretched hand.

"No, I don't want to." She rolls her eyes and a grimace tightens her mouth. "When is this damn thing going to start?"

Deflated, I sink back into the chair. It's not a big deal, just a stupid app, but my heart squeezes painfully as if it's a personal affront. Like she doesn't even care to learn this tiny thing about me.

"Can I see?" A low male voice sounds behind us, and I turn to find Austin Fielding, The Ole Aces bar owner. Scars pucker his face from time spent in the military, while his large frame barely fits the small folding chair he's seated in.

"What?"

He motions toward my phone. "Your listening personality. Learning about other people's preferences always fascinates me. Plus, the song that was playing is one of my favorites, so I'm curious to see how we match up. But if that's weird or..."

"No!" My body twists to face him more fully, though chamber members are taking their seats to start the meeting. "I mean, you can look, if you want. Everybody jokes about seeing the repetitive shares on social media, but I like seeing what people listen to, too," I finish dumbly, pausing on the second "too."

Try to act normal.

To be fair, I realize I'm pretty quirky for our small town—everyone thinks I'm named after Luna Lovegood from *Harry Potter* because of our similarities—but I'm working on toning it down around strangers. Not that Austin's a complete stranger. I've been to his bar a couple of times and our friends are dating, so we're aware of each other. But he tends to stick to himself.

"I'm Luna, by the way." In case he forgot.

A strange light enters his eyes as his lips quirk upward. "Yeah, I know who you are, Luna."

Oh.

"If we can have everyone's attention, we'll get started," Dr. Avery announces from his center position up front, and the room quiets. Austin returns my phone, his fingertips brushing mine as if we're in slow motion—each pinpoint of his touch eliciting a spark of recognition.

Heart sparks.

No, it can't be.

Suitor's Crossing has a town legend about finding your soul mate or *heart spark*, which I wholly believe is true, but surely Austin can't be mine. We've been in each other's company before and nothing happened. Yes, I find him attractive in a brooding mountain man kind of way, but that's not how *heart sparks* work.

Maybe it just requires a touch.

"First order of business..." Another chamber member reads down the agenda as I straighten in my seat, contemplating the burst of heat between us.

The possibility of discovering my *heart spark* consumes my thoughts the entire meeting.

Overshadowing my acceptance of the award.

Distracting me from my mom's attitude.

Is Austin Fielding the man meant to be mine—my *heart spark*?

CHAPTER ONE

AUSTIN

THREE MONTHS LATER

"If you fuck him with your eyes closed, then the scars don't matter. See? Problem solved." Triumph infuses the woman's voice behind me, and my fingers curl around the pen in my hand a little tighter.

For the past ten minutes, the trio of friends has contemplated the pros and cons of fucking the scarred bar owner of The Ole Aces—aka *me*. As if I'm not sitting right beside them in a separate booth. Sure, they have wooden slats that rise above the seats to create more privacy, but they aren't fucking soundproof.

Should've stayed in my office.

Except I barely fit behind the desk in there.

So, I hauled everything out here to the bar floor, commandeering a table that allowed me to spread out, but listening to biker bunnies bitch about my ugly face and then whisper about riding my dick isn't what I signed up for.

"You're right," Friend Number Two agrees. "It's not like we can skip him either. He's close with Snow, making him top of our list."

What the hell?

The mention of my best friend and the president of the Reaper's Wolves motorcycle club has me leaning forward against my better judgment. Since he moved to Suitor's Crossing, the bar's become a popular biker hangout. The guys come in to chill, then leave with the women here to experience a night on the wild side.

Fucking biker bunnies.

These chicks are clearly of that variety, but talk of a list is new.

"Yeah, but it's not like he's an actual member of the MC. Should he really even be on the list?" The last friend, the one who's done nothing to hide her disgust with my face this entire time, clearly isn't ready to admit defeat yet. "I say we move on to Fox and Timber. Forget Austin."

Alright, I've had enough of this shit. Her disinterest doesn't offend me; I'm used to women dismissing me these days after my face got blown to hell. But this is my bar, and I don't need to hear all about their plans to sleep their way through the entire roster of Reaper's Wolves members.

Sliding out of the booth, I round the barrier between our two spaces and order with a pointed finger in their direction, "Out. All of you. Now."

"What...?" Only one of them has the decency to look embarrassed for being caught talking about me, but the other two roll their eyes with a huff.

"You're kicking us out because we don't want to fuck Freddy Krueger?"

"No, I'm kicking you out because my bar has a 'No snobby bitches' policy. Effective immediately."

Customers snicker at a neighboring table, pulling out their phones to capture any more theatrics. Thankfully, the shame-faced girl grabs her purse and tugs on the woman beside her until the three shuffle toward the exit.

"Damn, don't run off all the biker bunnies, Fielding," someone calls from the back amongst a crowd of laughter. Ignoring the jibe, I return to my seat and try to focus on working, but the page of numbers swims before me as frustration courses through my veins.

I hate the attention my scars draw.

Hate how I've become either a fucked-up trophy to bed or a monstrous figure to avoid.

It didn't use to be that way. I wouldn't have called myself handsome before the explosion that wrecked my life, but women weren't actively put off by my appearance.

Now, it's the only thing they see.

The only thing I'm known for.

And it fucking sucks.

THE NEXT DAY

I SWEAR IF ANOTHER thing goes wrong with this place, I'm selling and moving to some beach paradise where I'm not constantly inundated with problems.

Sweat drips down my forehead and burns at the corner of my eye as I maneuver another barstool into place for Rhys to secure it to the floor. We've already finished installing eight stools with four more to go, and I'm fucking over this bullshit.

It's been over a year since I bought The Ole Aces, and just when I think I'm close to finishing renovations, some asshole comes in and decides to start a fight. Breaking my shit and shooting my insurance costs through the roof.

The Ole Aces has a reputation for cold beer, greasy food, and a rowdy atmosphere. I knew that going into the business deal. It's why the former owner parted with it so easily and at a reasonable price.

Situated at the edge of Suitor's Crossing, it's the perfect escape for the small town's grittier citizens, but since the arrival of the Reaper's Wolves MC, bar brawls have increased monumentally.

As club president, Logan, or "Snow," as his men call him, tries to keep the guys in line, but their tempers flare, fists start flying, and the next thing I know, I'm replacing barstools for the fourth time in two months.

At least they spend their weight in booze.

A major reason Logan relocated the club was to help me get the bar back on its feet. Military brothers for life, he's always had my back.

"Thanks to your *classy* clientele, you're quickly becoming my best customer." Rhys jokes, exchanging the drill in his hand for a bottle of water from the mini-fridge behind the bar.

"Shut it," I say with little heat. This time around, I requested a sturdier design made with thicker wood and more metal to hopefully prevent easy damage. Rhys's blacksmithing skills are well-known throughout Suitor's Crossing and the surrounding area—his craftsmanship leagues ahead of the local competition. So, it's not the quality of materials I'm buying that's shit. It's the giant pricks who come in swinging their fists, and anything else they can grab, at each other.

"I'm just saying... You'd think as your best friend and president of the Reaper's Wolves MC that Logan would keep a tighter leash on his men."

"You know as well as I do that the troublemakers are prospects, and they're dealt with accordingly. Besides, it's not them who start the fights most of the time anyway. These asshats come in with the intention of proving themselves to the big bad MC. It's a big pissing contest."

"That you're in the middle of." He points the top of his bottle toward me before downing half its contents.

He's got me there.

And the truth's fucking annoying.

Most of the members of Reaper's Wolves are former military like me and Logan—good men just looking for a home and brotherhood after serving their time. But there will always be bad seeds, guys looking to prove themselves, and that's where the trouble's been brewing lately.

We continue with the installation until the bar doors swing open to let in a ray of sunlight, followed by the familiar tinkling voice of Luna Haven. "Knock, knock! I know you're technically closed right now, but Willow said that Rhys would be here. I've got your spare phone charger."

Luna, Suitor's Crossing's resident free spirit, glides across the wooden floor in painted converse shoes. Whether it's butterflies or sunflowers, she always wears a unique pair to express her creative personality, and I'm mesmerized like every other time I've seen her around town.

Wonder if she paints them herself...
You could ask.

Except whenever I'm near Luna, my mind shuts down and my tongue gets tied into a thousand knots. Because she's full of light and energy that makes me want to hide in the shadows as much as it draws me in.

The one time I actually worked up the courage to speak to her was last December during a Chamber of Commerce meeting—something I only went to because I saw she'd be receiving an award. Then I sat behind her and heard her mom's dismissive tone, and the need to comfort Luna overcame my reluctance to speak to her.

It had been a glorious minute with her.

God, I'm fucking pathetic.

"Thanks." Rhys grabs the black cord dangling from Luna's hand and plugs it into a socket by the register to immediately charge his phone. "Something went haywire last night causing my phone to not charge, so this is a lifesaver. Are you headed back to the bridal shop to see Willow again?"

I avert my face as Luna nears. She pats one of the stool seats experimentally before hopping onto it and bracing her elbows on the gleaming wood of the bar. "Nah, I don't have plans for the rest of the afternoon. How many more of these do you have left to install?"

The curve of her ass sticks out as she starts twisting on the stool, her jean-clad legs swinging in the air. She's fucking adorable, and I wish I could go up behind her and wrap all of those soft curves in my arms.

But she's beautiful and bright, and I'm not.

After an ill-fated explosion in the desert, burn scars riddle my body—the worst of it decorating my face with tough raised skin that's a shade darker than my natural coloring.

"We're almost done. In fact..." Rhys glances toward me with a smirk, and apprehension slickens my gut. *What the fuck's he got up his sleeve?* "I can finish this last one myself if you want to check out Austin's office in the back. He can use your help organizing things, even if he won't admit it."

"The hell?" I mutter under my breath, but it gets lost as Luna drops to her feet with an exuberant smile.

"Really? I've been searching for another project after finishing the software updates at Brewed..." My reluctance must register because Luna's happiness dims and caution enters her voice. "But I don't want to overstep. If you've got a system that works for you, there's no need for me to mess with things."

I hate that cloud in her eyes. Hate that I'm the reason.

Rhys is paying double for his drinks for the next fucking month.

"No, I could use the help if you're free. Follow me." My head ducks down again, allowing my shoulder-length hair to fall forward and block part of my cheek from view. It's gotten easier dealing with people's stares since the accident, but I don't want to risk seeing a look of disgust cross Luna's pretty face if she sees them this close.

Especially after the ordeal with those women last night.

Fucking Rhys.

I remember last month when he came in complaining about *heart sparks* after meeting Willow and wonder if that conversation has anything to do with this.

Because I'd said a good woman could be hard to find.

That I envied our buddy, King, since he found the love of his life.

Was Rhys playing matchmaker by shoving Luna and me together?

Like she'd fall for you.
Not a chance in hell.

CHAPTER TWO

LUNA

Finally!

Ever since my brief interaction with Austin at the Chamber of Commerce meeting, I've yearned to explore the heat I felt when our hands touched, to figure out whether it was *heart sparks* or not. But every time I've visited The Ole Aces with the girls, Austin's hidden away in his office or too busy with customers to be bothered by me.

Maybe Willow said something to Rhys, and this entire thing's a set-up.

When she'd asked me to drop off the phone charger this afternoon, a frisson of excitement shot through my veins at the prospect of seeing Austin again. And now, thanks to Rhys, we'll potentially be working together—providing ample time for me to explore whatever this connection is between us.

You don't even know if he feels it, too.

My gaze travels the lengthy journey from his booted feet to broad shoulders as I match my shorter strides to his longer ones. His attention's focused ahead rather than on talking with me, and it seems unlikely that he feels the same attraction.

Damn.

Since December, we've been in the same room a handful of times, yet he still hasn't said more than a word of greeting to me. It's difficult to imagine this giant mountain man being shy, which leads me to believe *I'm* the problem—my personality is too much or something.

Not a happy thought when thinking of my possible *heart spark*.

Especially when my family limits their time around me, too.

You're working on improving. Just offer to help him, and don't get too crazy excited with suggestions.

"This is it." Austin opens the door to a cramped office full of papers stacked on a desk and a filing cabinet. The two of us barely fit in the room, so I'm impressed he manages to work in such a tiny space considering his enormous size.

"Wow, okay, this isn't quite what I expected, but I can work with it," I say, easing past Austin. It's awkward for a moment as I inwardly curse my wide hips and ass. Our bodies are flush against each other until he steps back to let me pass freely, a quiet apology muttered under his breath. "Do you just need me to file all these papers or would you like me to digitize things...?"

Austin runs a hand through his wavy hair, and my fingers itch to do the same, wondering if the shiny strands are as soft as they look. This man intrigues me like coding for a new app or piecing together a website. He's quiet, keeps to himself, and is clearly a hard worker since his focus has been fixing up The Ole Aces this past year.

The chaotic part of my mind—the side that never stops working, always finding something to dream about or create—likes the idea of his calming nature in my life. Other than following my thoughts into whatever project they deem worthy at the time, I've never really found anything to ease the hectic race my thoughts run. Which is why I have two degrees and a bunch of random entrepreneurial ventures.

Most people think I'm flighty or irresponsible because I don't stick to one job, but the truth is I love variety. Thanks to selling a popular app after college graduation, I have the funds to support myself no matter how I choose to spend my time. The gigs I take on around town are for a nominal fee. One, so people don't feel like they're accepting charity, and two, so I can evade questions from my family on how I support myself.

Since I never told them about my influx of wealth.

Who knew how lavish their gift lists would become if they realized money was no object?

"I'm not really sure," Austin mumbles, stuffing a hand in his pocket. "Rhys kind of sprang this on me, so I wasn't really expecting anything. You mentioned updating the software at Brewed, and you got that Chamber of Commerce award for helping small businesses. I trust your judgment. What would you recommend?"

The fact that he remembers seeing me three months ago boosts my spirit.

At least you're not forgettable. That's one point in my favor.

"Well..." I sigh, drawing a finger along the wall of peeling paint. That's got to be a health hazard. Ideas of what this room could turn into flash in my mind. "Do you want the extravagant Luna vision or the basic doable plan?"

His brows quirk to the center of his forehead, and the overhead light shines on the dark pink of his scars. Do they still pain him? Whispers of a military accident have floated around town, and I'm desperately curious to learn more about him—his past, and his future goals for the bar.

"The extravagant Luna vision, for sure. Tell me what you want to do."

Smiling in approval of his choice, I begin, "First off, this space is too small for you. It can't be comfortable. What's on the other side of this wall? Storage? If we can expand the room, I think you'll be much happier. Then..." Words tumble out of my mouth almost faster than I can think of them, at times my tongue tripping over the sentences until I take a breath and slow down, only to speed up again as excitement takes over. Once I'm finally finished, I lean against his desk with a relieved exhale and wait for his decision.

For someone who had this entire project hoisted on him out of the blue, he's accepting it fairly well. Maybe I shouldn't have even brought up the option of tearing down a wall—*wasn't I determined to tone down my wild ideas?*—but really I couldn't let him continue working in this dinky office without mentioning the possibility of expanding.

It's not like he's done renovating the rest of the bar yet. Why not add something for his own comfort?

Because perhaps he doesn't want another major overhaul tacked onto his list of chores?

Immediately, I regret suggesting a typical Luna option—a sane person doesn't jump to demolishing entire walls when asked to help organize an office. Trying to backtrack, my back straightens as contrition enters my tone. "You know what? Forget I said anything... Let me organize these files, digitize them, and..."

"Hang on, what happened?" Austin strides nearer and cups my cheek, an air of hesitancy surrounding him before concern overrides it. "One second your eyes are sparkling with joy about redoing the office, now they're dull with... regret? I understand if you don't want to tackle this project. It's a huge commitment after one afternoon, but you seemed up for the challenge."

"I am." My admission flies out without preamble. *Pause. Think. Breathe.* "But you're right. It's a big undertaking that you weren't expecting. Rhys probably thought I'd offer to organize your file cabinets, not completely demo your office. I'm sorry for going crazy and..."

"Hey," he growls low, breaking my shame spiral with the intensity in his voice. "Don't apologize for being enthusiastic, and don't criticize yourself for being creative and idealistic. I like you the way you are, Luna Haven. Like your ideas. Like the way your mind sees a problem and works to find a solution."

"You do?"

"Hell, yes." His fingers tap my cheek before retreating. The loss of his calming touch affects me more than expected. It was only a few seconds, but our connection grounded me. Reminded me of the brief graze of his hand back in December. "We're doing the big Luna vision because *you're* right. I need more space. I'll call the guys at Olson-Keller for the demo job, then we can get together to solidify your plans. Sound good?"

Sounds amazing.

That thought remains unvoiced, though, as I smile and nod before we leave to rejoin Rhys. No one's ever jumped headfirst into supporting my ideas like Austin. Sometimes people express doubt until I convince them it's in their best interest. Or if they're really stubborn, I rewind and offer a safer solution.

Which is why I'm trying to reign in my creativity and harness it into a manageable beast that people understand.

But Austin doesn't want the watered-down version of me.

And that feels damn good.

"HEY CALEB, HOW ARE you doing today?" The owner of Brewed lifts his chin in greeting and shrugs his broad shoulders as he fills a mug with hot coffee. "Same as always. You?"

"Oh, you know, keeping busy." *Waiting anxiously for a call from a certain bar owner.*

It's only been a few days since Austin agreed to let me redo his office. He probably hasn't even scheduled a demo crew to come in yet, but I'm itching to get started, to spend more time with him.

"Thanks again for your help. I still can't get over how quickly you set up our website and store. The online orders have been pouring in, and it's not even freaking me out because you made it so easy."

Blushing at his compliment, we chat for a few more minutes before I thank him for the coffee and head over to the corner table where Willow and Shannon are already seated. "Hiya!" I sit down, shrugging off my coat and purse.

Immediately, Willow leans forward, her palms flat on the table and a gleam of mischief in her eyes. "Rhys tells me that you and Austin are working together... *alone.*"

"Not exactly," I say, shaking my head at her obvious interest. Willow is a romantic at heart, and although Rhys was the exact opposite when they met, *heart sparks* eventually won out—with a little help from the app I created, of course. He's head over heels in love with my friend now.

"Alone or not, the fact is you two have 'forced proximity' now."

"Oh, a trope! You are definitely reading too many romance novels," Shannon cuts in with a laugh.

"And you're clearly not reading enough." Willow pointedly glances down at Shannon's left hand, where her engagement ring sits, despite the issues we've seen between her and her fiancé. Granted, I haven't seen a lot, but Willow's filled me in on the basics. Shannon used to be happy, and now she's not. Something's been off in their relationship for months, according to Willow, who spends every day with Shannon as her employee at the bridal boutique.

Apparently, she and Hannah have decided enough is enough, voicing their concern over Tim, a man they don't believe is Shannon's *heart spark*.

"We're not having this conversation again," Shannon huffs, turning defensive. "Between you and Sierra, it's a neverending cycle."

Guess her best friend Sierra's in on the intervention, too.

Before our coffee date grows too tense, I guide the conversation away from her and Tim. "Has Rhys heard anything from Austin? He hasn't reached out about finalizing things yet, so I wonder if he changed his mind."

"He hasn't. Asa and Rhett drove down from High Ridge yesterday to tear down the wall themselves, since they're friends with the guys. Rhys came home sweaty and covered in dust last night. My guess is Austin will call you soon."

Buzz!

On cue, my phone vibrates with an incoming text, and a splash of coffee lands on the table after I jolt in response. Willow and Shannon laugh at my jumpiness, but I ignore them to read the message.

Unfortunately, it's from Uncle Rob instead of Austin.

Rob: *You still coming tonight? Your cousins would love to see you, and I know your mom would, too.*

It takes all my strength to keep a straight face at his false sincerity. The only reason he wants me there is to foot the bill, I'm sure. Otherwise, I probably wouldn't be invited.

Unless there's a financial component to an event, my family tends to leave me out. They don't understand me, most of the time brushing me off as annoying, which really fucking hurts.

And is the reason behind a ton of my issues—why I haven't told them about my wealth, why I constantly search for a project they'll approve that will make them proud to be associated with me.

Yeah, my therapist has a field day during our sessions because I'm a mess.

"Guessing that's not Austin?"

"Nope. But it's okay." I play it off with a forced smile, although they can read between the lines to my disappointment. "As Willow said, I'm sure he'll message me soon, and we'll get started. No big deal."

If he doesn't contact me before tonight, I might seek him out instead, since my uncle recommended the Ole Aces for his birthday. I could casually bump into Austin and gauge where his head's at.

Easy.

Suddenly, I can't wait for tonight.

CHAPTER THREE

AUSTIN

Luna's seated in a corner booth with a group of people—her mom, her uncle based on the greetings I heard, and two cousins. I don't recognize her extended family from my visits to town, but it appears they're just like her mom.

Dismissive of Luna.

Earlier when she came in with a bright smile and a large gift bag, her uncle had snagged it without a word of thanks before proceeding to openly complain about the bag's contents. Watching Luna slowly wilt in her seat with each derisive comment had my body itching to go over there and teach the prick some manners.

Especially when no one else at the table seemed likely to. Her mom agreed with the insults while her cousins played on their phones.

"Uh-oh, has another one bit the dust with this *heart spark* shit?" Logan asks, pounding my back with his palm. Tearing my gaze away from Luna, I bite into the hamburger in front of me without replying, although the muscles tense around my neck and shoulders.

Cole, a local handyman and friend, laughs. "It's about time another brother falls. Figured you had something for Luna based on how your eyes never leave her whenever she's in the room."

Hopefully, she hasn't noticed my obsession. I'm sure finding out the scarred freak of Suitor's Crossing can't stop ogling you isn't part of her *heart spark* dream.

This idea of *heart sparks* originated from one of the town founders over a century ago. He crossed a bridge with the girl he liked, and they were in love by the end of the journey. Married soon after. Soulmates for life. Thus the *heart spark* myth.

It's not that I don't believe it's true. I have friends who are living proof of its existence: Rhys, King. I'm just not sure it'll work for me. I'm not native to Suitor's Crossing, and the myth has a lot to overcome with my looks.

Not that I think Luna is shallow, but a pretty girl like her would never fall for a scarred man like me.

"It's not *heart sparks* if it's not reciprocal," I mutter after swallowing my bite of dinner.

"How do you know it's not reciprocal?" Logan cuts into his steak and stares me down.

"Have you looked at me lately?" I raise a finger to my face before grabbing my bottle of beer and taking a swig.

"Not every woman is a superficial bitch. She could like the warm, cuddly teddy bear you are on the inside," he jokes, although a note of seriousness enters his voice. Logan was there when I got wounded and knows what I went through to heal. He also knows the trouble I've had with women since finishing all the surgeries to fix my face.

Well, to make it semi-presentable at least.

"I'm not saying Luna's superficial, but she can do better than me. Besides, you've been around King, Rhys, and their women. *Heart sparks* aren't subtle. If I were hers, don't you think we'd know it? She's not exactly shy. Luna would announce it to me straight on, and she hasn't yet, which means that we're not. End of story."

"What I find interesting is that you said 'if I were hers,' instead of 'if she were mine,' which makes me think that you *do* believe she's your *heart spark*. But you're too afraid to learn how she feels." Cole smirks, and if he wasn't giving me a friend's discount with the repair bills he sends me for fixing things around the bar, I'd wipe the smarmy grin off his face with my fist.

"It doesn't matter what I do or don't believe. It's not gonna happen for us." No matter how much I want it to.

Do I think Luna is my *heart spark*?

Hell yes, I've known for a while.

From the first moment I saw her enter my bar, I knew. But it was also obvious that I'm not good enough for her.

Who wants a man that everyone gawks at? A scarred beast who still wakes up in the middle of the night with nightmares from the incident that cost me so much?

No one, that's who.

I would never burden Luna with my baggage. So, no matter how much I adore her, I'm determined to adore her from afar.

Even with Rhys pushing us together for this whole renovating my office fiasco. I'll let Luna do her thing to make her happy, and then we'll go back to the way we were before. Seeing each other occasionally when she comes to the bar with her friends or at random events when our friends invite us out, but that's it.

"Oh, guess what?" Luna's excited voice carries over the din of conversation to our table. "I received a letter in the mail today about a—"

"It's getting late. My friend's laundry is probably dried and needs folding before I drop it off tonight." The elder Ms. Haven grabs her purse—completely ignoring her daughter—and glares expectantly at Luna. "You need to move so I can leave."

"Bitch," Logan mutters under his breath, and I couldn't agree more.

"Now? Can't it wait another ten minutes? This is really exciting—"

"No, I don't have time to hear you rattle on about some odd gig you picked up. Have you looked at any of the job openings I sent you? They're looking for operators at the call center."

Soreness radiates from my jaw because my teeth are clenched so tight. A call center? Luna's leagues ahead of an entry-level job answering phones all day. There's no shame in the work, but my girl's got a mind brimming with creative ideas. A place like that would stifle her to death.

Before I realize it, my chair scrapes across the bar floor as I push back, ready to defend Luna, but then her uncle and cousins pile in with excuses for leaving. Two seconds later their table's empty aside from Luna and, conveniently, the check for everyone's meals.

Are you fucking kidding me?

The guys chuckle as I desert them and march over to my girl. Sliding the check across the table away from her, I say, "You're not paying that. It's on the house."

"Austin, where'd you...? Never mind. Stupid question, since you own the place."

"Which means you aren't required to pay this." The slip of paper goes into my jeans pocket before I sit across from her. "So, that was your family, huh?"

Luna flushes. Her strawberry cheeks match the cute red fox on her shirt. "Yeah, you might remember my mom from the Chamber of Commerce meeting. Then her brother and his two children. We're celebrating his birthday tonight."

"That's nice." I try to keep the annoyance out of my voice and fail miserably based on her wry grin.

"I take it you overheard some things?" A nervous laugh follows my nod of confirmation.

"Just a couple. But it was enough for me to see they don't appreciate you."

Luna's shoulders rise and fall with a resigned exhale. "They just don't understand me. I've always been different with my wild ideas and overenthusiasm. They wish I was more like them, and I do, too, most times."

"I'm glad you're not like them," I admit, warming to the subject. For some reason, it's becoming easier to talk to her; I'm not so tongue-tied.

Probably because you're still pissed at her family.

"There are a lot of people in the world like your family. The ones who don't have the imagination to dream of a better future for themselves or the people around them. We all need people like you who aren't afraid to break the mold and build a better world."

"You make me sound like some sort of superhero." She smiles before adding, "I think I like it. I just need a superhero name."

Willing to ease into a lighter topic, I relax into my seat, tossing an arm across the back of the booth while I contemplate her adorable features: silver blonde hair threaded with blue in two messy buns, a dimple in her round cheeks. Damn, she's beautiful.

"Moonbeam. You shine a light on the dark areas in people's lives."

"That's really sweet and matches my hair." She tugs on one of the strands left down to frame her face.

We sit in silence for a moment, unclear on where to go from here, until Luna crooks a thumb towards the back of the bar. "Willow mentioned earlier that you demoed the office already. Can I see it since I'm here?"

"Sure." *I'd love to have you all to myself.*

Without a crowd of onlookers hanging onto our every word.

The short trip to the office is marked by the chuckles of my friends as we pass their table, and I know they're going to tease me mercilessly later.

"Here we are."

The overhead light switches on to reveal the empty space. Everything's been cleaned up since me and the guys tore down the wall separating my former office from a storage space.

Luna walks the perimeter of the room, plans, no doubt, flying through her mind like shots fired from an AK-47. Unerringly, her hand smoothes over the patchy paint job, and I can practically read her thoughts.

"We need to repaint the walls before moving my desk back in. Do you have any colors in mind?" I expect a list of paint colors to tumble forth but she remains silent. "What? No suggestions for bright pink or green?"

Joyful laughter erupts as she shakes her head. The carefree sound wraps around my heart and squeezes. "No, no, no. You don't want to be distracted by flashy colors here. You need a calming atmosphere that promotes focus. Something like a soft blue or maybe a cream."

"We can head to the hardware store tomorrow if you're free."

"Sounds like a plan. Although I loathe supporting Joe after how he treated Hannah."

Remembering how Joe forced Hannah to work through lunch breaks to the point where she became ill still raises my ire, despite knowing she's in a healthier place now with King.

"Me, too. That's why I figured we could drive to High Ridge's hardware store. It's a little out of the way, but at least we'll be supporting a local business that's not run by an absolute prick."

Luna quickly agrees, and we stand staring at each other in silence—both of us waiting for the other to speak—until squeals of raucous laughter interrupt us all the way back here. It breaks the awkward moment.

Guess my loss of speech around her isn't completely gone, after all.

"I should let you get back out there to make sure the crowd stays civil." Luna edges by me, and the giving curves of her body mold to my front, tempting my cock from its semi-hardness to full mast.

Fuck, I hope she doesn't notice.

"With the Reaper's Wolves, civility might be asking too much." We slowly head back down the hallway to the main bar floor.

"You know them pretty well, right?"

"Yeah, Logan's one of my best friends. We served together."

"For how long?" At the end of the hall, we stop, both of us turning to face the other as we lean on opposite walls. I cross my ankles in an effort to hide my erection, though the motherfucker's too large to be completely disguised.

"Eight years in the army, so we've known each other for twelve years total. It's kinda wild when I think about it." Logan's been by my side for over a decade, a true brother in arms.

"Right? That's how I felt when we had our high school reunion a few years ago. Some of those people have been in my life pretty much since grade school. It's weird because we grew up together and know certain things about each other. But now we've gone down various paths, so we're different, too... I don't know... I'm just rambling." A nervous chuckle ends her thoughts as she pulls at a hair tie around her wrist, twisting it over and over again.

"No, I get it. It's like my injury. There's an Austin before, and now we're in the after. At least your journey's been positive so far, right? With the whole town award and everything?"

Luna perks up and finally stops fiddling with the band. Good thing, too, because I was about to remove it after watching her delicate skin turn pink from the fidgeting. "Speaking of awards, do you want to hear about the letter I got today? I'm dying to share with someone."

"Lay it on me."

"Someone nominated me for the Washington Medal of Merit, and I won. They invited me to a dinner and awards ceremony at the end of the month, where the governor will bestow it upon me."

"Holy shit." Obviously, Luna's amazing and Suitor's Crossing already recognized her for her service to the community, but this is huge. This is a commendation from the entire state for her work and generosity.

"That's an understatement. No one mentioned nominating me, so I'm extremely grateful." The corners of her eyes crinkle with happiness as she shrugs. "Not that I need awards or anything, but it's nice to hear when you're appreciated. Even if it's done anonymously."

I wish she didn't need to rely on strangers for encouragement, though. Her family's doing a shitty job loving her, that's for sure.

So, take over.

Give her what she needs.

As Luna continues to elaborate on the award and its criteria, my heart and mind decide that's exactly what I'm going to do.

Consequences be damned.

She may not want me like I want her, but she needs someone in her corner. Deserves all the love and support in the world.

And I'm going to give it to her.

CHAPTER FOUR

LUNA

A ustin's funnier than I expected.

We spent the day in his truck, driving to and from High Ridge's hardware store, and our conversation never faltered. He'd make dry comments about this or that—funny tidbits which had me laughing and relaxing with him in ways I haven't with men in the past.

The only awkward times were when we were actually in the store around people. Austin clammed up and kept his chin down, face averted to hide his scars.

I hated that he felt the need to obscure his looks from the public. But after one wayward customer caught sight of him and gasped in shock, a wrinkly hand covering her chest, I understood why he felt it necessary.

I wouldn't want to deal with everyone else's reactions either, especially with something I clearly felt insecure about. It's odd thinking of Austin as insecure about anything with his giant frame and confident attitude inside his bar, but it endeared him to me even more. Which is saying a lot considering I already feel halfway in love with him, and we've barely spent time together.

About to spend more together, too, painting the walls a fresh cream color. Excitement adds an extra skip to my step as we enter The Ole Aces and head to his office.

"Oops, I brought the wrong bag of paints," I groan, reading the labels on the bottles in my canvas tote. Despite visiting the hardware store, I decided to bring one of my crafting bags from home for touch-ups or fun accents. Except this bag holds an entirely different set of supplies.

"You have more than one bag of paints hanging around your house?" Austin asks, a smile playing about his mouth.

"Apparently." Kneeling on his office floor, I dump everything out into a haphazard pile. "These are body paints."

He joins me on the ground and studies a bottle of red paint, reading the label with scrunched brows. "Why do you have so many body paints? Is it leftover from Hearts Ablaze?" The mention of the town's annual February festival of love is a good guess because I do volunteer to paint faces, but these were bought with a very specific purpose in mind.

A hopeful purpose.

"Nope. These are meant for couples. It's from a company called Body of Love. Basically, couples paint each other as a fun activity." And a sexy one, too, I muse as my gaze drinks in Austin's muscular body, imagining my hands sweeping over the vast expanse of his skin.

Shadows darken his expression as he carefully sets the bottle down. "Couples? This is leftover from an ex?"

"God, no!" I've never been brave enough to use them, especially since I wanted it to be a special occasion with my *heart spark*. "An ad for them sucked me in. I bought them in the hopes to share them with someone in the future. See? The plastic wrappers aren't even broken yet."

He has the decency to look embarrassed as I flick one of the quality assurance plastic wraps with my fingernail. "Sorry... my mind jumped to you and another man, and I got..."

"Jealous?"

Thick lashes hood his amber eyes before one growled word sends a shower of sparks cascading down my spine.

"Yes."

It's what I've been waiting for—an admission of something from Austin to prove I'm not the only one feeling this intense attraction. Perhaps his jealousy should be a turn-off, but for a girl who's either been dismissed or unfairly judged all her life, I'm living for the possessive way he feels about me. Reveling in the knowledge that a quirky, curvy girl like me could elicit a reaction from a burly mountain man like him.

Kinetic energy pulses from the tips of my fingers down to my toes, a chaotic mass of atoms urging me forward, until I'm close enough to feel the heat of Austin's breath on my lips.

"Good." My mouth ghosts over his before I lean back on my calves and search his expression. Did I push too hard too fast? Was I too bold?

"What are you doing, Luna?" The whispered rasp raises goosebumps on my arms as his large palm slides over my cheek, the rough skin catching on the baby fine hairs. Consternation lines the part of his forehead untouched by scarring, while the rest of his face tightens, highlighting the differences in texture and color.

Hesitantly, I trace the path of a particularly angry-looking scar and Austin shudders. My hand jerks away, afraid of causing him more pain. "Does this hurt?"

"Not anymore..." A shaky breath rattles from his chest. "But I don't expect you to touch them. I know how ugly they are."

"They're not ugly." The denial immediately spills out—hating that he views himself that way. "You bear the scars of a warrior. When I look at you, they don't scare or disgust me because they mean you went through hell and survived. You became stronger and should wear them with pride. But you're more than what we see on the outside. You're brave and kind—a successful businessman who has a community of people who care for him."

"I doubt Suitor's Crossing thinks much of me after drawing the Reaper's Wolves to town," he scoffs, trying to turn his face away, but this time, I cup both of his cheeks and hold his gaze. I'm sure if he tried, he could break free—after all, he's twice my size—but it's obvious how desperately he wants to believe me.

For all his bluster and confidence when he's working, I'm thinking my big mountain man may be missing a few necessities in his life. Like warmth, affirmation, and love.

"I meant me, Willow, and Rhys, the entire Reaper's Wolves MC. Hell, probably most of The Ole Aces patrons, too. You're not alone. You're not some defective freak." That might have been too harsh but I push onward. "You're Austin fucking Fielding! Hot as hell mountain man and ex-military to boot. Is it any wonder I've wanted to kiss you for forever?"

"Yes, actually, though my brain's trying to catch up." One of his hands strokes his bare chin where the scarring obviously prevents hair growth. "Mountain men usually have beards, though."

Of course, that's what he decides to comment on.

"Some do, but it's not a requirement. You're a man and live on a mountain. Doesn't get much clearer than that. Now, as far as my feelings, would it help if I drew my desire out for you?" I pick up a bottle of blue body paint and tear away the protective plastic before squeezing a tiny dot on my finger. The ingredients say they're safe for sensitive skin, but just in case, I figure we can start slow... if Austin agrees.

His eyes ping-pong between the paint and my face. "Is this part of your extravagant Luna vision?" he teases, an unfamiliar emotion softening his body.

"Going with my gut and winging an impromptu intimacy session with my potential *heart spark*? Yep, sounds like it to me."

"You think I'm your *heart spark*?"

I wince. "Is that too much? We've only just kissed and..." The paint on my finger begins to spread into a round glob, underlining how ridiculous I must seem. Austin likes me, but does that mean I need to fast-track toward love and *heart sparks*?

A normal woman wouldn't.

At least, I assume she wouldn't, since I've never been labeled "normal" in my life.

All of a sudden, Austin's hands grip the back of his tee and pull it over his head, revealing a wall of muscle decorated with more scars. The breath hitches in my lungs as his vulnerability—and tough sexiness—sinks in.

"Paint away, little moonbeam."

CHAPTER FIVE

AUSTIN

If someone told me I'd be laying shirtless before Luna, waiting for her to trace my scars with paint-covered fingers, I would've laughed in their face.

Reveal the ugly patches marring my skin to my adorable *heart spark*? Fuck no!

Yet here I am, vulnerable in a way I never expected to be for my curvy little moonbeam.

The wood flooring at my back cools some of the nerves firing through my system, and I'm damn glad the bar's closed until later tonight. I don't want anyone interrupting wherever this is leading.

Luna hesitates a moment before straddling my waist, carefully easing her weight down on my hardening cock. "Is this okay? If I'm too heavy..."

"You're not. You're perfect." My fingers dig into her love handles and rock her body into mine. The irony of encouraging Luna to accept perceived body flaws isn't lost on me, but her curves are natural and beautiful. My scars aren't.

"If you say so." A shy grin peeks out at me before she raises her finger with the blue dot of paint. "I'm going to start small at first to make sure you don't have a negative reaction. Let me know if anything burns or itches, and we can stop."

I shiver at the first touch of wet paint. She's gentle with her movements as if she expects me to stop her. Little does she know that she's filled my dreams for months now, so feeling the soft sweep of her skin along mine? It's damn near heaven.

"Feel alright?"

"I'm good," I choke out. Luna's touch is electrifying. It's as if her finger is a magic wand sweeping over my cheeks, neck, and chest, anywhere she can reach, and she exchanges painful memories for golden ones I never want to forget.

The zigzag leftover from shrapnel? A swooping signature of Luna's tenderness.

That crisscross of nasty cuts? Exes and ohs. Hugs and kisses from my sweet girl.

"Baby, I need to see you. To touch you, too." My hands tug on her shirt, wordlessly urging her to take it off and show me my prize: her lush tits that jiggle with each of her movements.

"Yes, please..." Immediately, she complies, ripping her shirt overhead, uncaring about dirtying it with paint.

With her bra soon tossed aside also, Luna bends forward, allowing her breasts to rub against my scarred chest and smear the paint between our bodies. It's an odd sensation and sexy as fuck, but I crave more.

My restraint is gone. My reservations dust in the wind.

"Take these off, too, then give me some paint." The demand rings clear in my voice. I've let her explore, and it's my turn to reciprocate. This has been my dream for months. I don't want to waste another second not knowing the silkiness of her skin beneath my fingertips.

As she wiggles around to follow my directions, I kick off my jeans and boxers, my cock rising upward like a steel pole pointing toward the sky.

"Here's yellow—my favorite color." Luna distractedly gives me the small bottle, eyeing my erection.

"Sit on it," I rasp in eager arousal before common sense barges in. "Unless you're not ready. That's fine, too. I just needed to be free before I busted my jeans' zipper"

"Oh, I'm ready." Luna returns to her previous position with both thighs caging my hips before sliding her pussy over my cock, getting it nice and wet like the dirty girl I imagined she'd be. No way a woman as creative as my Luna couldn't be a little wildcat in bed. "Healthy and on birth control. You?"

"I'm clean." Can't remember the last time I slept with another woman, honestly.

Content with my answer, a sexy little moan zings through the air as she works the tip of my cock into her cunt before sinking lower in one slow motion that has my muscles tensing with control.

Goddamn, she's hot. Tight. So fucking wet for me.

"Fuck, you gonna ride me, moonbeam? Gonna pump this dick with that sweet cunt of yours until I fill you up with my cum?" I squeeze dollops of the yellow paint into my palms and immediately reach up to pinch her nipples. Their budded tips, coated in the blue paint from my chest, beckon me like sirens of the sea.

So, I pinch and tug, our individual colors blending into a deep green while I hold her bouncing breasts captive as surely as her pussy clenching on my dick.

"Mmm, Austin..."

"What do you need, baby?" I tweak her left nipple a little harder and spank one of her juicy ass cheeks, growling at what my handprint on her ass means.

Possession.

Ownership.

The cutest little growl of frustration rumbles from her throat like a disgruntled kitten, and she shrugs, swiping a sweaty strand of hair off her face. "I don't know. More? Harder?" She tries to initiate something new with the swivel of her hips when I flip us over.

"I know what you need." My paint-colored hands immediately spread her thighs wide as I dive into her cunt, my tongue spearing through damp curls to tease her clit. Luna bucks upward with a gasp. Her fingernails scratch at my scalp, and there's no doubt I'll find blue flecks in my hair later tonight.

But I don't give a fuck.

Because I'm eating the sweetest pussy I've ever tasted—pleasuring my girl the way she needs, the way I've imagined loving her for a long fucking time.

The wait was definitely worth it.

CHAPTER SIX

LUNA

"Yes, fuck... Austin, don't stop." Mindless pleas ring in the humid air, our combined body heat turning the office into a verified sauna. I'm so hot, sweat forms between my breasts and beads on my forehead.

Austin keeps his face buried between my thighs, obscene grunts of pleasure rumbling from his throat.

This isn't how I imagined our afternoon going, but I can't say I'm disappointed. My body's been on edge all day.

Every time we'd brush against each other or I'd catch him staring at me like I was the last piece of cake at a birthday party, lust careened through my blood and straight to my pussy.

And finally, Austin's doing something about it. His tongue curls upward and pumps into me before he nudges my clit with his nose. He's making the most of what he has available since his hands are covered in paint, and it's totally working for me.

"Goddamn, this pussy is so sweet. You were made for me, weren't you, little moonbeam? Made to come on my tongue before I stretch this tight cunt with my cock."

"Yes, yes..." A loud moan bounces off the walls, an orgasm firing its way through my veins like a raging forest fire.

"That's right. Give me all that pussy cream, baby. Your little clit needed some attention first, didn't it? Needed my tongue before your pussy sucks my cock dry. Isn't that right?"

He doesn't wait for an answer, just flips me to my stomach and slams his hips forward. I yelp at the instant fullness of his thick cock burrowing deep, and my hands search for purchase on the floor as I slide forward.

Austin's arm wraps around my waist and hauls me backward with a displeased growl. As if I was trying to get away, and he didn't like it.

Like I'd abandon the raw fucking he's giving me.

I'm not *that* crazy.

"Fuck, I love your pussy." Austin smacks my other butt cheek, and I imagine matching handprints on my ass. Signs of my man's loving.

Mmm... my man.

I like the sound of that.

The angle changes as he adjusts his body to mine, hitting that sweet spot inside that lights me up like a freaking Christmas tree. Too soon, another shout of satisfaction bursts out of me as the tension breaks, pleasure raining down like a million shooting stars, and Austin follows suit, a harsh growl accompanying his release.

Like a limp ragdoll, I remain splayed out on the floor, weak from my intense orgasm. Who knew an accidental body paint mishap would lead to this? Being fucked by hardworking giant, Austin Fielding?

A sensual shudder races down my spine at the reminder of his tongue, his big hands, and his ironhard cock.

A cock that he's only now pulling out, much to my dismay.

God, I want him again. And again. Not just because he's some mountain man sex god, but because he's my *heart spark*. There's no doubt in my mind after the day we spent together chatting and shopping and then fucking like a pair of wild animals.

You should ask him now.

"Will you be my date to the governor's gala when I get my medal?" The question spills out of my breathless body. I wanted to ask him yesterday after sharing the news but worried that once again, I might be moving too fast, too soon.

However, considering our current circumstances, it seems we might actually be on the same page regarding this relationship.

Except Austin stiffens above me.

"The governor's gala? Like a black-tie event?"

"Yeah, it's formal, but if you don't have a suit, I'm sure we can—"

"That's not the issue."

"But there is one?"

He rolls to a sitting position, all of his painted scars and muscles flexing under the fading afternoon sunlight streaming through the window. "It's going to be a special night for you. I'd just be a distraction. Everyone will gawk at my face instead of celebrating your accomplishment. I don't want that for you."

Relief floods my veins as my neck and shoulders lose some of the rigidity his hesitancy caused. He's trying to think of what's best for me. His conclusion is wrong, but it's still sweet.

Heaving my body upward, I try not to focus on being naked and having this conversation.

Impeccable timing, Luna.

"What other people do doesn't matter to me. I want you with me because I'm proud to have you by my side. I'm used to stares because of my quirky personality. This won't be new or bothersome."

"It'll bother me." The seriousness in his tone tells me there's more to this than he's letting on. I study the thinning of his lips, the downcast set of his eyes.

He's concerned about upstaging me, yes.

But I'm guessing there's an aversion to being the center of attention at such a high-profile event, too.

My heart breaks for him. And for myself. Because I won't force him to go. I don't want to cause him more pain, even if it hurts knowing I'll be attending alone. Sure, one of my friends will probably agree to tag along, but a part of me felt full—whole—thinking Austin would be there to support me.

Swallowing past the lump in my throat, my chin dips down as I blink away a wave of tears threatening to fall. "I understand. You're right. I'll just tell you about the night afterward."

"Baby..."

"It's fine, but what's not fine is the mess we made. We should probably clean up before the bar opens." It's a terrible segue, but what can I say?

He made up his mind, and I don't want to sway him with my tears. So, I'm going to buck up and move on. Starting with all this paint.

Remembering an industrial sink back in storage, I head that way, encouraged when I hear Austin follow. We'll get past this. It's not a deal breaker for me.

It's just a disappointing moment.

Luckily, my family's given me plenty of practice dealing with them.

CHAPTER SEVEN

AUSTIN

It's Friday night, and the bar is rowdy as hell with bikers and old-timers drinking and playing pool. I shouldn't be working. I should be with Luna at the awards gala.

But you're a fucking coward.

These past few weeks with Luna have been better than I ever imagined and more than I deserve. She's quirky and funny, sweet and generous. Not to mention sexy as fuck and good enough to eat, which I do every damn day.

We finished my office with new shelving and a larger desk to accommodate my big frame. Everything was chosen with my comfort in mind, thanks to Luna.

I love her.

Then what are you doing here?

I scrub a hand over my face, focusing on the rough texture of my scars. They'd draw attention tonight. Guests would stare and ignore Luna.

A cold sweat forms on the back of my neck. For all the strides I've made toward accepting my scars—ignoring people's opinions—it seems a ballroom full of politicians, business owners, and other influential citizens is my limit.

There's a reason I chose to settle in Suitor's Crossing. It's a small town in the mountains. Remote. And while I'm comfortable with bar patrons, this is different.

Is it?

Luna will be by your side, and you know she doesn't care about what other people think or do.

The clock ticks in the background. Four thirty-seven. She's probably getting ready right now, preparing for the drive.

"Fuck it." I can't let my girl go alone, no matter how uncomfortable I'll be. Luna needs me, and I promised to show her the love and support she deserves.

And I almost failed the first test.

"You better hope you pulled your head out of your ass in time." An old suit hangs in my closet at home. I just need to shower and change before heading over to Luna's and apologizing for my idiotic behavior. She's been so understanding since I turned down her original invitation. The subject hasn't come up again, and I regret that she might have felt like she couldn't share her excitement for the event because of me.

Several bar patrons try to stop me on my way out, but I politely decline their advances, determined to get to Luna as soon as possible. The exit's a few feet away when the doors swing open and her mom walks through with another lady.

You've got to be fucking kidding me.

She'd rather bar-hop with a friend rather than support her only daughter. What a bitch.

"You're not welcome here," I grit out, stepping in front of the older woman to prevent her from going further.

"Excuse me?" Her friend inches away, avoiding eye contact.

"You. Are. Not. Welcome. Here." Each word is controlled and firm. "Luna's being recognized by the governor tonight, yet you choose to drink with a friend over supporting her? Well, not at my bar. Luna's mine and you best believe she comes first. Which means not enabling your miserable behavior as a mother. Now leave before I have someone escort you out."

Ms. Haven cackles. "If she's so important to you, then what are you doing here? Seems like the pot calling the kettle black to me."

I hate that she has a point. Thank fuck, I came to my senses before she arrived.

"The difference between you and me is I realized my mistake and plan on rectifying it." One of Logan's men from Reaper's Wolves sidles up to the side, and I nod toward Luna's mother. "See that she leaves. I've got a date tonight."

And I leave without a backward glance.

My girl's alone and needs her man.

And a big ass apology.

CHAPTER EIGHT

LUNA

It looks like I'm attending the prom I never went to. From the puffy sleeves of my Selkie gown to my converse shoes.

Not much has changed in my life since then. I still have an unsupportive family who wouldn't be able to afford the cost of tonight's gala like we couldn't afford my ticket to senior prom.

Not that they were interested in coming to the gala when I invited them, anyway.

On the bright side, my love life's improved. Austin is amazing, even if he isn't escorting me to the awards ceremony. His fear is valid. People probably will stare, and I understand why he doesn't want to be in the limelight.

Still sucks going alone, though.

Mom backed out last minute.

Uncle Rob went out of town on a fishing trip.

And my cousins all moaned and groaned about feeling out of place at such a fancy event.

Like somehow I'm better equipped to handle that environment on my own?

A resigned sigh puffs past my lips as my head tilts back, my eyes rapidly trying to blink away tears. Tonight's supposed to be a celebration—a joyous occasion.

The doorbell rings.

I'm not expecting anyone since I'm going alone, but maybe one of my family members decided to surprise me. A flutter of hope kindles in my stomach, and I rush to grab my purse and jacket before opening the door with a whoosh.

Instead of my mom or cousins, it's Austin standing in front of me in a nice suit, hair tied back, and a bouquet of roses in his hands.

"What are you doing here?" Shock wars with elation. We just texted an hour ago with him congratulating me again.

"I'm here to apologize and escort you to the gala. You deserve to have everything you want in life, including me as your date for one of the most important events of your career." He takes a deep breath and continues, "I'm sorry I let my insecurities get in the way of that at first, but I'm here now to support you, Luna Haven. Because I fucking adore you and—"

He doesn't get any more words out because I throw my arms around his neck and smash a kiss against his lips. The bouquet of roses smashes between our chests, the crinkling of the plastic wrapper a dull sound in my ears.

Austin came for me.

I understand his concerns, but he overcame them *for me*.

"I love you, Austin," I blurt out. He's my *heart spark* and deserves to know how I feel, however irrational the timing may seem.

"Glad you finally caught up, moonbeam. I've been in love with you from the moment we first met."

Our lips meet again, this time a possessiveness entering Austin's embrace.

"You should've said something," I mumble, unwilling to break our connection too much.

"I thought you deserved better than a scarred veteran like me. But as I was sitting alone at the bar, contemplating the dumb mistake I made refusing your invitation, it occurred to me that no one's gonna love you better than me. No one could possibly adore every perfect, curvy, creative part of you." He punctuates the promise with a nip to my bottom lip and a squeeze of my ass.

"Is that so?"

"Damn right. Now, let's go get that Medal of Merit so I can eat this pussy when we get home. I've got some making up to do, and you're gonna feel it come tomorrow morning."

Smiling, I smack his shoulder before sashaying away. "Can't wait."

EPILOGUE ONE

AUSTIN

TWO YEARS LATER

"**W**hat the hell is this supposed to be?" Cole studies the canvas framed on the wall in our living room, an expression of bafflement furrowing his brow. Luna and I share a secret smile as I shrug in response.

"Don't know."

It's the first body paint intimacy session we did as husband and wife, and Luna figured we should showcase it since it actually did turn out like a piece of artwork. Sometimes it feels like we singlehandedly keep that company in business as often as we use their products.

We've even tried playing with creating different shapes and color schemes. Throughout it all, Luna and I laugh like crazy before passion overrides anything but fucking each other's brains out.

"Hope you didn't spend much on it," Cole mutters, and I stifle a chuckle behind my fist. *If only he knew...*

"You don't like our painting?" Luna teases from the kitchen where she's finishing the website for Cole's handyman website. I join her at the table, wrapping an arm behind her back and kissing her shoulder.

"Shame. We had quite a time creating it." The murmured words are for her ears only as I nuzzle into her neck. Today she's wearing a bright pink skirt with a shirt covered in tiny unicorns to match her converse. On anyone else, it might look ridiculous or childish, but my girl pulls it off.

Luna marches to the beat of her own drum, and I happily follow her lead.

"Hmm... we did. Our next order should arrive tomorrow. A special glitter set that I can't wait to use."

"You don't need glitter, moonbeam. You sparkle well enough on your own."

She rests her head against my arm and smiles. "You're too sweet to me."

"Sweet? Austin?" Cole snorts and interrupts the moment. "Sorry to break up the flirting, but I wanted to remind y'all I'm still here."

"How could we forget?" I drop a quick kiss on Luna's lips, ignoring his groan of amused frustration. I'm gonna kiss my wife any damn time I please, especially in my own home.

It took me too long to claim Luna for my own two years ago. I let fear hold me back from my *heart spark*. So, I don't mess with that shit anymore and let my girl know how I feel every day, whether it's through words or actions.

She's my bright moonbeam, and I'm determined to never see her light dimmed ever again.

EPILOGUE TWO

SHANNON

"Congratulations, you're going to be a beautiful bride."

"It must be great owning a bridal shop and being a bride. You get the first pick of new gowns!"

The cacophony of good wishes and congratulations weighs on my shoulders as my bridal shower wraps up. This should be one of the happiest days of my life, soon to be replaced by the actual happiest—my wedding day—but I can't shake the feeling of discomfort that's settled over me these past few months.

Like a grey cloud heavy with rain, it sinks deeper and deeper over me until sometimes it feels like I'm wading through a sea of fog. Aren't brides supposed to be bright-eyed and bushy-tailed?

No, those are squirrels.

But they should at least be excited to marry their fiancés. As the owner of Blushing Brides Boutique, I've heard my fair share of love stories, yet mine... doesn't feel the way those women described.

Geez, what's wrong with me?

Whatever it is, I need to fix it quickly because I will be Mrs. Tim Grantham in less than a week.

Unless I shouldn't be?

Tim finally proposed six months ago, and I try to remember how happy I felt. I'd dropped hint after hint about rings and potential wedding venues while our moms followed suit, constantly asking the direct question of when will we get married and start popping out grandbabies.

He always shrugged with a secretive smile, and I humored his reluctance. Chalking it up to his determination to build his career rather than a marriage at the time. Hell, I've been doing the same thing with opening Blushing Brides Boutique.

Starting a small business in a small town isn't easy, but Suitor's Crossing's legend of love factored into my decision to build here rather than in a larger city.

Heart sparks or soul mates abound in Suitor's Crossing. We have a romantic bridge from over a century ago where the myth originated—cross the bridge and you'll soon meet the person meant to be yours.

Or if you're already in a relationship, you'll know if they're your *heart spark* or not.

I can't say I've been brave enough to cross it with Tim.

We work so well together. Both driven and ambitious. Our parents are great friends and practically arranged our marriage long before Tim's family moved to Suitor's Crossing and we first met.

We make sense.

Even if our relationship lacks the sparks or magic that my friends have found recently.

Willow and Rhys.

Hannah and King.

Luna and Austin.

The list goes on and on.

As they like to remind me.

"Ugh! Stop doubting your decision. It's done. You're getting married next week at noon," I berate myself, causing my dachshund, Melon, to lift his head from its resting position and stare questioningly at me.

"That's right. I'm becoming Mrs. Tim Grantham today, and you're our ring bearer, and everything will be perfect."

So, why does it feel like I'm trying to convince myself to walk the plank of a pirate ship?

DON'T MISS SHANNON'S STORY NEXT IN
MARRYING THE MOUNTAIN MAN**!**

THANKS FOR READING & DON'T FORGET TO RATE/ REVIEW!

Please consider leaving a rating/review. Ratings & reviews are the #1 way to support an indie author like me.

The more reviews, the more my books are shown to other potential readers!

And they serve as guides to readers on whether to take a chance on an indie author.

I appreciate your support!

XO, Hallie

BOOKS BY THIS AUTHOR

Every Hallie Bennett book features a curvy girl & a
filthy-talking hero!
Find Hallie's entire catalog at www.thearrowedheart.com!

ABOUT THE AUTHOR

Hallie prefers steamy, insta-love stories where curvy girls are claimed by filthy-talking heroes. And when she ran out of reading material, she decided to write her own stories. If you want a quick, hot read, she's your girl!

www.ingramcontent.com/pod-product-compliance
Lightning Source LLC
Chambersburg PA
CBHW050320200626
46812CB00019BA/2923